The Secret
of the
Painted House

The Secret
of the
Painted House

by Marion Dane Bauer
illustrated by Leonid Gore

A STEPPING STONE BOOK™
Random House 🏠 New York

Text copyright © 2007 by Marion Dane Bauer
Illustrations copyright © 2007 by Leonid Gore

Published in the United States by Random House Children's Books, a division of Random House, Inc., New York. Originally published in hardcover by Random House, Inc., in 2007. First paperback edition 2008.

Random House and colophon are registered trademarks and A Stepping Stone Book and colophon are trademarks of Random House, Inc.

Visit us on the Web!
www.steppingstonesbooks.com
www.randomhouse.com/kids

Educators and librarians, for a variety of teaching tools, visit us at
www.randomhouse.com/teachers

The Library of Congress has cataloged the hardcover edition of this work as follows:
Bauer, Marion Dane.
The secret of the painted house / by Marion Dane Bauer ; illustrated by Leonid Gore.
    p.   cm.
"Stepping Stone book."
Summary: When her family moves from Chicago to the country, nine-year-old Emily is drawn to a mysterious playhouse she finds in the woods and soon meets its sad, lonely inhabitant.
ISBN 978-0-375-84079-1 (hardcover)
ISBN 978-0-375-94079-8 (lib. bdg.)
[1. Playhouses—Fiction. 2. Haunted places—Fiction. 3. Brothers and sisters—Fiction. 4. Moving, Household—Fiction. 5. Illinois—Fiction.] I. Gore, Leonid, ill. II. Title.
PZ7.B3262Sec 2007   [Fic]—dc22   2006024829

ISBN 978-0-375-84080-7 (pbk.)

Printed in the United States of America

10 9 8 7 6 5 4 3 2 1

First Paperback Edition

Contents

1

The Playhouse

Emily pushed out the screen door and let it slam behind her. She stood on the top step, gazing in every direction. *Trees! Nothing to see except trees!* Why did her parents think she would love it here?

This place was just a few houses set in a patch of trees. Beyond the trees stretched Illinois cornfields. The nearest town, where Emily would go to school when school started, was miles away. The nearest kid must be miles away, too, except for her little brother.

But Logan didn't count. He was four years old. When you are nine, a four-year-old is almost a baby.

"I'm going," she called back over her shoulder.

"Going where?" Her mother came to the door.

Emily shrugged. Where was there to go? "I guess I'll check out the 'forest.'"

That's what Logan had called it yesterday. "Cool," he'd said when they'd pulled up behind the moving van. "We're going to live in a forest!"

But "cool" was hardly the word for this bunch of trees.

"Okay," Mom said. She sounded a little

uncertain. "Just be careful, will you? Don't go too far."

Emily sighed. At home in Chicago, Mom worried all the time. She was afraid someone might snatch Emily off the sidewalk. What was she going to worry about here . . . bears?

Emily set off without looking back. She didn't need to. She could "see" her mother in her head. Mom was hot and tired. Her dark, springy curls were pulled into a ponytail. Her T-shirt was wrinkled. Moving a whole house was hard work. Boxes waited everywhere. Last night they had to search for sheets before they could fall into their beds.

This morning Dad had gone to his new job. Before he went, he'd told Emily, "Be sure to help your mom." And she *was* going to help. But not just yet.

Emily stepped off the gravel road into the

trees. The leafy branches closed around her.

She rubbed at the goose bumps that sprang up on her arms. Should she go back? But then she thought of the piles of boxes. That kept her moving. This was just a patch of woods, after all.

The land sloped down, so she followed the slope. At the base of the hill, a creek bubbled over a stony bed. Emily stopped at the edge of the water. Maybe she should go back. She had promised her father. And she didn't much feel like wading.

But then she saw stepping-stones. Flat stones crossed the creek right in front of her. She stepped onto the first one. It was solid. The next one wobbled a bit. The one after that was steady again. She made it all the way across the creek without even wetting her sneakers.

The other side of the creek was the same. It was trees and more trees. Why cross the creek to see more trees? The creek itself would be fun to play in, though. Maybe she could bring a friend to play. But she had no friends here.

Emily was about to turn back when she glimpsed something white. What was it? Even staring hard, she couldn't tell. White seemed an unlikely color to be part of a tree or bush. She made her way toward it.

She didn't know what to expect. Certainly not what she found.

A house stood in a small clearing. It was a real house, but small. Maybe it was a child's playhouse. A girl her size could walk right into it. A grown-up would have to duck to get in through the door. The walls were painted white. The roof, the door, and the shutters at the windows were a rich royal blue.

The playhouse wasn't new, though. It had been standing here for a long time. The white paint had peeled. One blue shutter hung crooked. A branch had fallen and punched a hole in the roof.

A rusted padlock held the door shut.

Emily tried the handle, anyway. She couldn't help trying it, even though she could see the lock. The lock hung there, saying, "Keep out!" The playhouse said something else. It said, "I've been waiting for you for a long, long time. Please come in!"

Of course, the door didn't budge.

Emily circled the house. She found no other way to enter. The shutters were all closed. She circled a second time. As she circled, she opened each shutter. When they were all open, she peeked inside.

Emily had already begun to imagine what she would find. A table and two chairs? A tiny sofa? A toy piano? Maybe a sink and stove for the kitchen.

In her mind, everything was made just to fit. But her fantasy was wrong. There was nothing. Inside, the playhouse was empty.

She cupped her hands around her eyes and pressed her nose against the window. And that was when she saw something more wonderful than child-sized furniture.

Beyond the empty floor rose the walls. But these walls were special. Every single one was painted from top to bottom in a picture.

Emily moved from window to window. She checked every wall. What a strange picture it was! The walls were covered with trees. It was as if the woods around the playhouse had moved inside!

She tried one more window. Still, she saw trees, only trees. Trees grew outside. Painted trees grew on the walls inside. But wait! She spotted something else now. Something white showed through the painted trees. White, with a blue roof.

A playhouse stood in the painted forest, too. The painted playhouse looked exactly like the one she was peering into!

Emily backed away from the window. A small shiver scurried down her spine. How odd this all was! A playhouse in the woods. Woods inside the playhouse. A playhouse inside the woods inside the playhouse! If she could look through the windows of the painted playhouse, would she find more woods? Would she find another playhouse?

The idea made her dizzy.

2

See a Pin and Pick It Up

Emily didn't tell her mother about the painted house. She didn't know why exactly. The whole thing felt too new to talk about, and too strange.

Besides, her mother would worry that the playhouse belonged to someone. She would say Emily shouldn't have peeked in the windows at all. She would certainly say that Emily shouldn't go back.

Emily spent the rest of the morning unpacking boxes. Logan even helped . . . if it could be called "helping." He emptied boxes with lightning speed, but he didn't put anything away. Not even his own toys.

Once Emily caught him tucking a box of matches into his pocket. When she took them away, he howled. Logan loved matches. He had even learned to light them. He was the kind of kid who had to be watched every minute. Anything he wasn't supposed to mess with thrilled him.

Lunch was bottled juice and peanut butter and jelly on crackers. Mom hadn't found a grocery store yet.

After lunch Mom put Logan down for a nap.

"I'm going to lie down, too," she said to Emily. "I'm tired. Do you want to rest?"

Emily shook her head. "I'll read," she said.

She took her book out to the front steps. It was a ghost story, one of her favorites.

But before long she put it down. She'd read it several times, and it was getting boring. The ghost showed up in the same place every time. And the girl seemed pretty dumb to be so surprised to see it. Hadn't she gone into that old house looking for ghosts?

Emily didn't know what else to do. Go back to the playhouse? She couldn't without telling her mother. Besides, it was a long walk, and the afternoon was growing hot.

A woman with white hair came out of the house across the way. She wore white slacks and a flowered blouse. She wore a smile, too. The woman smiled all the way to Emily's porch.

"You're Emily," the woman said.

It was more of a statement than a question, so Emily didn't reply.

"I'm Grandma Rose," she said. "That's what everybody calls me here—Grandma." She held out a hand.

Emily shook her hand. She felt funny doing it, though. Usually only grown-ups shook hands with each other.

"May I?" Grandma Rose asked.

At first Emily didn't know how to answer. *May I what?* Then she figured it out. Grandma Rose wanted to sit down.

"Sure." Emily scooted over to make room.

Grandma Rose settled herself. They sat there, side by side, looking off into the trees.

"My mom's taking a nap," Emily said. "Should I go wake her?"

"Goodness, no! Let her sleep." Grandma

Rose looked into her eyes. "It's you I came to see, anyway."

"Me?" Emily was so shocked that "me" came out as a squeak.

Grandma Rose nodded. "I saw you go off into the woods this morning. Did you find it?"

Find it? What was this woman talking about? But before she even had a chance to ask, Emily knew. "You mean the playhouse?"

"What else?"

Emily took a deep breath. "Yes. I found it."

Was Grandma Rose going to scold her? Maybe she wasn't supposed to go near the playhouse. Maybe it belonged to Grandma Rose or to some long-ago daughter of hers.

"It's . . ." Emily didn't know what to say about it, really. "It's nice," she said finally.

"Nice!" The word exploded with a laugh.

Emily stared.

"Weird would be more like it." Grandma Rose shook her head. "Built over there across the creek. Practically lost in the woods. All that painting on the walls."

Emily took a breath. "The woods inside the house," she said.

"And the house inside the woods," Grandma Rose added.

Emily sighed. She wasn't the only one who found the painting strange!

"It's like they go on forever," Grandma Rose said. "Each one gets tinier and tinier."

So Grandma Rose got the same feeling from the painting she did. "Who built it?" Emily asked. "Who was it for?"

"It was for Pin."

"Pin?"

"Her name was Penelope. Penelope Hanson. But folks called her Pin. 'See a pin and pick it up. All the day you'll have good luck.'" Grandma Rose paused. She seemed to be thinking.

Then she added, "She didn't, though. Have good luck, I mean."

Emily held her breath. She knew the beginnings of a story when she heard one.

"Pin's dad had money . . . as you might guess. Building a whole house like that for a child. Not that his money did him much good." Grandma Rose folded her hands in her lap. They were wrinkled in a friendly way.

She turned to Emily. "His wife ran off and left him, you see. She left them both. She was an artist—a painter. They say she went off to be with her own kind. She just left that girl behind. Nothing to remember her by but the paint on those walls."

So Pin's mother had done the painting. And then she had left. Somehow that made everything even stranger.

"What happened to Pin?" Emily asked.

"She died." Grandma Rose's voice grew soft. "Her dad's fancy mansion burned down, and she died in the fire. Some folks even said she started it. Nobody knows, really. She was just a girl, no older than you." Grandma Rose's eyes were a sad blue.

Emily leaned forward. "When did it happen? The playhouse and the fire? Was it a long time ago?"

"Yes. It was a long time back. In the fifties. They are probably all dead by now. It seems I heard about her mother dying recently. She must have been pretty old."

Emily looked around the small circle of houses. "So there used to be a mansion here."

"Right here," Grandma Rose agreed. She swept a hand to take in the whole area. "There used to be just one big house in all this space."

"And a playhouse," Emily added.

"And a playhouse," Grandma Rose agreed. She stood up and slapped dust off her white slacks. "I'm not sure anybody ever played in it, though."

There were a hundred questions Emily wanted to ask. A thousand, maybe. But she didn't know where to start. And before she could ask a single one, Grandma Rose was gone. She waved good-bye. Then she marched back across the gravel road.

3
Flowers for Mommy

"**W**here are you going?"

Emily turned back. Her mother stood on the porch. "Just for a walk. I won't be long."

Yesterday she had worked all afternoon. Today she wanted to see the playhouse again.

She *had* to see it.

Mom wiped her flushed face with the back of her arm. "I told you, Emily. I need you to watch Logan this morning."

"But—"

Her mother wasn't listening to any "buts." "I'm trying to set up the kitchen. And Logan is underfoot. You can go for a walk. Just take your brother with you."

"Mother-r-r!" Emily knew she was whining. She also knew her mother hated whining. But how could she explain? Mom needed her to watch Logan. But she needed to go back to the playhouse just as badly.

Emily had thought about nothing else since yesterday. Last night at dinner she'd had to bite her tongue to keep from blurting out her secret. That's all she had been able to think about . . . the playhouse.

The screen door snapped shut. Her mom had gone back inside. The argument was over. Her little brother waited on the porch.

Emily made a face at him.

Logan had dark curls like their mother's. He also had her huge green eyes. But Mom never stuck out her lower lip the way Logan was doing. If he started bawling, their mother would be out here in an instant.

What could Emily do? She couldn't take Logan to the playhouse. He was a blabbermouth. If he saw it, he'd tell Mom and Dad everything. Then she'd never be able to go there again. And she couldn't wait until his nap time. She simply couldn't!

"Come on," she said to Logan.

Emily took his hand. They came down off the porch and began walking. Emily didn't have a plan yet. She'd get one, though.

"Where are we going?" Logan asked. He dragged his feet through the dusty gravel.

"We're going to the forest," Emily said.

"What are we going to do in the forest?" Logan's sneakers sprayed gravel with every step.

Emily thought fast. "We'll get flowers for Mommy. Let's find some pretty ones."

Were there flowers in these woods? She

didn't know. Yesterday she hadn't been looking for flowers.

Logan brightened at the idea and picked
up his feet. That was good, anyway.

Emily left the road and headed into the
trees. He stayed close at her side.

"I have an idea, Logan," she said. "We'll
break up."

"Break up?" His forehead wrinkled. "What
are we going to break?"

"We're not going to break anything, silly.
We'll look for flowers in different places. I'll
take you to a special place where you can pick
flowers. Then I'll go on to another place and
find some more."

That should give her time to check out
the playhouse.

Logan scowled. "Why can't you pick
flowers in my special place?"

"We can find more if we look in two spots. Don't you think?" Emily held her breath. Would he agree?

Logan's face looked like a thunderstorm brewing. But as suddenly as his mood had gone bad, it got better again. He even took a little skip at Emily's side. "We'll get Mommy the prettiest flowers ever," he sang. "Won't we, Emily? We'll get her a big, big bunch. It'll be so big she'll have to use the bathtub for a . . . for a . . ."

"Vase," Emily finished for him.

He beamed. "For a vase," he agreed.

They came to the stream. Emily stopped at the edge. She didn't want to cross it with Logan. He might see the playhouse.

"Oh, look!" Logan cried.

She looked, holding her breath. Had he spotted it?

But no. Logan pointed at a clearing on this side of the stream. Violets dotted the grass.

She smiled down at Logan's round face. His cheeks were flushed. His eyes sparkled.

"Flowers for Mommy!" he exclaimed. He ran and dropped to his knees. He tugged at a purple flower.

In an instant he had half a dozen in his hand. The stems were only about an inch long.

"Not like that." Emily knelt beside him. "You have to get the stem, too. A long stem. As long as you can."

Logan nodded. Very carefully, he picked another. He pulled it up, roots and all. Emily didn't say anything. There were lots of violets in the clearing.

"I'm going to go find some more. For Mommy," she told him. She stood and looked down at her brother's dark curls. "I'll be right back. So you stay here. Okay?"

"Okay," Logan agreed. He didn't even look up when Emily slipped away.

It's all right, Emily told herself. *I won't be long.*

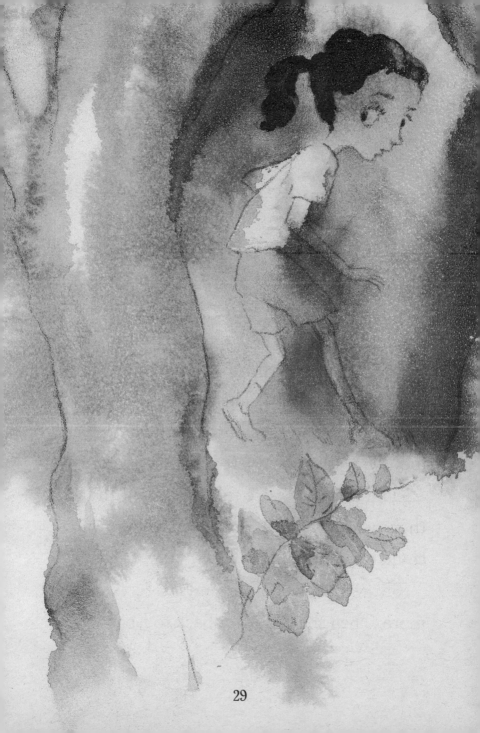

4

"Emily!
Please, Come Back!"

Emily stood back from the playhouse. She studied it carefully. The padlock still hung from the door. The shutters still were open, too. All was as she'd left it the day before.

The windows were tightly closed. In fact, they were the kind that didn't open. How could she get in?

She wanted to look around inside. Nothing more. Then she would go back to Logan. She tugged at the padlock. Some rust fell off. The door didn't budge.

At the front of the house, the windows were large and low. She wished she could open them. If she could, she could easily climb through.

She pushed on one of the windows. It gave a little. She pushed harder. The frame was rotten. Each time she pushed, the whole window moved just a bit.

She tried picking at the rotten wood. All she got was a splinter under her fingernail. The wood wasn't rotten enough for her to pull it apart.

Then she saw a fallen branch a few feet away. It was short and stubby. She tapped at the window frame. Nothing happened. She tapped harder. A few splinters fell off. She had to hit it harder.

She held the stick over her shoulder like a baseball bat. She swung at the frame. At least she meant to hit the frame. Her blow landed on the windowpane instead.

The glass shattered.

Emily gasped and dropped the branch. She had broken the window! She had broken somebody else's window! It wasn't even one that belonged to her parents!

A message flashed through her brain. *Run! Get far away . . . fast! Go get Logan and go home!*

And she did start to run. But then she stopped at the edge of the clearing.

She turned back and stared at the playhouse.

The window was broken. It was already broken. Nothing Emily did would change that. And no one else was here to see the window . . . or her.

She was alone.

She walked back to the playhouse very slowly. She stared at the broken window.

She had never done such a thing in her life. Logan broke a window once. He threw his wooden truck at Emily's bedroom window in their old house. The window had cracked from top to bottom.

But Logan broke lots of things. Especially, he broke things that belonged to her.

She looked at the broken window. Jagged pieces of glass stuck out of the frame. She would have to clear those away.

She picked up the stick again and began tapping at them. Finally, the frame was clear. Emily climbed through the window into the playhouse.

She crunched across the floor and stopped in the middle of the room. There was so much to look at. There were trees, of course. There was underbrush, too. She could see a rock covered with moss. Tiny yellow flowers peeked out from the roots of a tree.

And there was the playhouse. Emily moved closer. The playhouse in the painting was perfect. The shutters were straight. The white paint gleamed. No one had broken the front window. No one had put a padlock on the door, either.

Had Pin's father put the lock on after she died? Pin couldn't play in her playhouse. Maybe he didn't want any other child in here, either.

But Grandma Rose said it all happened long ago. Pin's father was probably dead. Even Pin's mother was dead. No one was left to care about this playhouse. No one cared that Emily was here.

Something caught her eye. She moved closer to the picture.

It was a painted picnic!

A red and white cloth lay beneath a tree. There were hot dogs on it. She could see ketchup and mustard, too. She could even see pickles. Potato salad filled a big bowl. Emily loved potato salad.

And here was a pile of marshmallows! You couldn't have a picnic without marshmallows.

A campfire waited to be lit.

Emily wanted to step into the wall. She wanted to sit down on the checked cloth and light the fire. She would pick out a marshmallow to roast. She touched one of the painted marshmallows.

And then she noticed the brush. It lay on one corner of the cloth. An artist's palette lay beside it. The artist might have just put them down.

The palette held all the colors of the picture. Red and green. There were lots of shades of green. Blue and yellow and white, too.

Emily's finger itched. She wanted to pick up the brush and add something to the picture.

Not that she could paint like Pin's mother.

But that's when she saw her. A girl was

painted into the picture, too. She peeked from behind a big tree. That's why Emily hadn't noticed her before.

Her blond hair fell over her shoulders in two fat braids. She wore a sailor dress. It was blue with white piping and a red tie.

"Are you Pin?" Emily asked the picture.

She didn't get any answer. She didn't really expect an answer.

The girl in the picture looked as if she wanted to speak, though. She looked as if she wanted to say, "Who are you? What are you doing in *my* playhouse?"

"I'm Emily," Emily told her. But then she took a step backward, away from the wall. It was silly to talk to a picture.

Besides, she had to go. Logan had probably pulled up every violet in the clearing by now.

She wouldn't come back here again. This place gave her the creeps.

She was climbing through the window when she heard her name.

"Emily," a voice said. It was as clear as if it came from someone standing right behind her. "Emily! Please, come back!"

5

Into the
Painted Woods

Emily spun around. She stood still, trying
to catch her breath. Then, slowly, she eased
back inside the playhouse.

She didn't know what else to do. She
couldn't run away. Why would anyone run
from a picture?

Or a voice. Where had the voice come
from, anyway?

She looked in every direction. There was

no one. Real trees outside. Painted trees inside. The real playhouse. The painted playhouse. And, of course, the girl in the picture. Emily had seen her behind one of the trees. Which tree was it?

Emily looked at one painted tree, then another. The girl simply wasn't there.

She looked around wildly. She hadn't made a mistake. The girl had been there. She had been behind that tree . . . the one to the left of the playhouse.

And now there was nothing. Just a patch of crushed grass where someone might have been standing.

Farther back, a bit of red poked out from behind another tree. It looked like the hem of a skirt blowing in the wind. But the girl hadn't been wearing red.

A chill crept up Emily's spine. The skin at

the base of her skull felt bunchy and tight. She turned, once more, to leave.

This wasn't happening. It couldn't be. She had only imagined seeing the girl in the painting. She had imagined someone calling her name, too.

She wasn't leaving because she was scared. She had to get back to Logan. It was important to get back to Logan!

"Emily!"

This time the voice came from another side. Emily jumped. She whirled to face the painting on that wall. And there the girl was. She stood in full view now. She was inside the painting, but in front of the trees.

"Yes," Emily said. She tried to sound calm. Still, her voice shook.

"Come here. Come in here with me," the girl said.

"I . . . I don't think I can," Emily said. "I mean, you're . . . and I'm—" She stopped. Was it polite to remind someone that she was dead? Or only a picture? Which was it, anyway?

The girl laughed. "Never mind that," she said. She crooked a finger. "Come on in."

Said the spider to the fly, Emily thought. But she said, "How?" Had she missed some kind of door into the wall?

"Just close your eyes," the girl said.

"Close my eyes," Emily repeated. Her eyes refused to close. She went right on staring at the girl. "Then what?"

"Just close them," the girl said again. "Tight. Then come here to me."

Emily forced her eyes shut. She took a step toward the wall. A small one.

"Come on," the voice begged. "Don't

think about the wall. Think about the picnic we'll have."

Picnic, Emily thought. She took another step. She could feel something. At least she thought she felt something. It bumped against the toe of her sneaker. Another step and her face would be smunched into the wall.

"Keep coming," the voice urged. "You're almost there."

Emily took a deep breath and another step. Then another. Then one more.

Everything around her went still.

Her eyes flew open.

She wasn't inside the little playhouse any longer. She was among the trees. The painted trees. And the girl stood right in front of her, grinning.

"You made it!" she cried. "You're here!"

"Am I really inside . . . ?"

"Inside the picture? Of course you are. You're in my world now. And you're going to stay!"

That startled Emily. *You're going to stay.* She hadn't said anything about staying. But she would worry about that later. Now she asked a more important question. "Are you Pin?"

The girl's grin widened. "Sure thing. That's my name. 'See a Pin and pick it up . . .'"

"'All the day you'll have good luck,'" Emily finished for her.

The grin faded. Was Pin annoyed that Emily knew her little rhyme?

"'See a Pin and let it lay,'" the girl added, "'bad luck will follow all your day!'" The rhyme was beginning to sound like a threat.

Emily took a step backward. She bumped into a tree. She put a hand behind to catch herself. The bark felt . . . well, it felt painted.

What would Pin feel like if Emily touched her? Would she feel painted, too? Emily didn't want to find out.

Pin's eyes were sparkling again. They were an icy blue. "Come on," she said. She began threading her way through the trees.

At first Emily stood there, watching Pin go. She wasn't sure she wanted to follow. But she didn't want to be left behind in the picture, either. She hurried to catch up.

"Is anyone else here?" she called after Pin. "Does anyone else ever visit you?"

Pin shook her head. "Just you," she answered. She didn't look back. "No one else has come for a long time." She kept up a steady pace.

So other people had visited. Probably long ago. "What happened to them?" Emily called

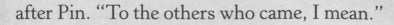

after Pin. "To the others who came, I mean."

Pin said something Emily didn't quite hear. It sounded like "They got away."

"What?" Emily called. She stopped walking. Her throat had gone tight.

Pin turned back and spoke more clearly. "They went home," she said.

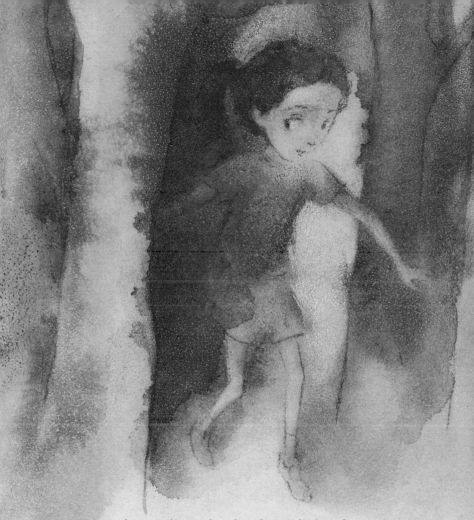

Was that what she had said the first time? Still, she said it so matter-of-factly. Emily began walking again.

She followed Pin into the painted woods.

6
Marshmallows

Pin stopped in front of the playhouse. Emily stopped beside her.

I'm inside the picture, Emily told herself. But it was hard to believe. The painted playhouse stood before her. It seemed solid and real.

It seemed as solid and real as the one she had broken into. But here the blue and white paint was fresh. No padlock held the door shut. The front window was unbroken.

Emily peeked inside. These walls were covered with trees, too. The trunks were like bars on a cage. Was Pin in this picture? Was she inside the cage of trees?

If she was, Emily didn't want to meet her. She had a feeling that one Pin was enough.

She turned back to the Pin beside her. "I left my little brother," she said. "He's picking flowers. I can't stay."

It was true. She had left Logan alone too long. What if he wandered off and got lost?

"You *can't* go!" Pin spoke so sharply that Emily jerked.

"Why not?" she asked.

"Because . . ." Pin glared. Was she angry? Or was she just determined to get her way? "Because you've got to have a picnic with me first."

Emily almost laughed. Almost. But she looked at Pin's face and didn't. The girl was serious.

Pin came closer. She glared harder. "I've even got stuff for s'mores," she said.

"Uh . . . sure." Emily loved s'mores. Who didn't? What about Logan, though?

But what could happen to Logan? He called this a forest. Really, it was only a small patch of woods. Even a four-year-old boy couldn't get lost in it. And how many people had ever had a picnic inside a picture?

Still, Emily wasn't sure. Were they going into this wall, too? It was one thing to step inside a picture. But to step into a picture inside a picture?

"Come on," Pin said. And she turned to leave.

Emily followed, relieved. She followed Pin

outside to where the picnic waited for them.

The red and white cloth lay on the grass. There were hot dogs, mustard and ketchup, and pickles. There was potato salad, too.

The makings of the s'mores that Pin had promised were there, too. Marshmallows sat in a pile next to graham crackers and chocolate bars. But where had the graham crackers and chocolate bars come from? Emily hadn't seen them before.

Off to one side, a tepee of small sticks waited to be lit.

The only thing missing was the artist's palette and brush. Where had they gone?

Pin picked up a stick. She poked it into a marshmallow. "For you," she said. Then she handed the stick to Emily and pointed toward the unlit campfire.

The stick felt odd in Emily's hand. It was

smoother than a twig from a tree should be.
And it had no weight. She looked at the unlit
campfire.

"Are you going to light it?" she asked.

"No!" Pin answered. She said it sharply,
her face suddenly pale.

"Why—" Emily started to ask.

But Pin broke in. "No fires."

Then Emily understood. Of course! Pin had died in a fire. She must be afraid of fires. Even a little campfire scared her.

So Emily held her marshmallow over the tepee of sticks. She was already pretending the painted marshmallow was real. She could pretend there was a fire.

Pin did the same.

The silence was so heavy it made Emily's ears hurt.

"Do you live here in the playhouse?" she asked finally.

Pin seemed surprised. "No, of course not! My dad's house is over there." She waved a hand in the direction Emily had come from.

A shiver ran beneath Emily's skin.

"And your mother?" she asked. She kept her voice calm. She pretended this was a normal conversation.

"She's here. She went away once. But she's here now." Pin said it fiercely. She seemed to think Emily might argue.

"Have you seen her?" Emily asked.

Pin shrugged. "She plays hide-and-seek. She loves hide-and-seek. Only"—her voice caught—"I can never find her."

A sudden cramp brought Emily's hand

across her stomach. She looked around. What was that flash of red she had seen in the woods earlier?

Was Pin's mother somewhere inside this picture? But why wouldn't she let Pin see her?

Pin's voice brought Emily back. "You'll stay, won't you?" It was half question, half demand.

Emily didn't know how to answer. She pulled the marshmallow off her stick. And then she held it, amazed. The marshmallow had puffed and toasted to a light brown. And it had done that over an imaginary fire!

It was as if someone had painted it anew.

But Pin wasn't paying any attention. "You've *got* to stay!" she said. It was an order this time.

"I—I can't," Emily stammered. She was

still staring at the toasted marshmallow. "My mother . . . We just moved here, and you see . . . I . . . I have to help her."

The moment she said it, she knew it was a mistake. She should have found another excuse.

She could have said, again, that her little brother was waiting. She could even have said that she had to go home to her father. That would have been okay. But she never should have mentioned her mother.

"Well." Pin's voice was hard. "I wouldn't want to keep you from your mommy."

Emily's cheeks grew hot. She scrambled to her feet. She still held the marshmallow. It didn't matter what Pin said. This girl couldn't keep her here.

She turned to go. To her surprise, Pin was right in front of her. She had been sitting by the unlit fire. Now she stood in Emily's path. How had she moved so fast?

Pin didn't say anything. She just stood blocking Emily's way. Her face looked fierce.

"I told you." Emily started around Pin. "I've got to go."

"You can't go." There Pin was in front of her again.

"What do you mean? I can't go?" Emily was so amazed she almost forgot to be scared.

"I mean, you're in my world now. You have to stay."

Emily's scalp prickled. Was it possible? Once she came into the picture, was there no way out?

Still, she said, "I don't *have* to do anything!" The words came out sounding braver than she felt.

She stepped in another direction. Pin was right there again. How could she get away from her?

"Move!" Emily ordered.

Pin didn't. But she didn't look angry now.

She just looked sad. "I need you," she said. Her voice was soft, pleading. "I need . . . someone. I get so lonely waiting for my mom to come back."

"But I don't want to stay here," Emily told her.

Pin shrugged. Clearly she didn't care what Emily wanted.

Emily tried once more to step around her. It didn't work.

"Emily!"

Emily caught her breath. The voice came from far away.

It was Logan! It had to be Logan. She must go to him.

"I'm coming!" Emily called. "Logan, I'll be right there."

She began to run. She didn't try to step around Pin. She just ran straight ahead.

And suddenly Pin wasn't in front of her.

Had she managed to run past the girl? Or had she blasted right through her? She didn't have any idea.

She kept running.

The grass caught at her feet. She almost tripped over a tree root. Suddenly the ground was rough.

Birds chirped overhead.

The air stirred around her.

Emily looked down at her hand. She still held the marshmallow. Or it had been a marshmallow.

Now, white paint oozed between her fingers. White paint faintly tinted with brown.

7

Logan!

Emily couldn't hear Logan calling anymore. She kept running all the same. At the stream, she didn't bother looking for the stones. She just splashed across it. She came to the clearing.

This was where she had left Logan picking flowers. She knew it was the place. But he was gone.

The grass was trampled. Most of the

violets were beheaded. But her brother wasn't here.

"Logan!" she called.

There was no answer.

"Logan!" she yelled again, even more loudly.

Still silence.

Where had he gone? Back home? Would he know his way back home?

She started up the hill. She would check at the house first.

But then she stopped. What if he wasn't there? What would she say to her mother?

If she went back without Logan, what would Mom say to her?

Emily turned down the hill again. He had probably tried to follow her, anyway. She retraced her steps.

Back at the playhouse, she didn't see any

trace of her brother. And he had stopped calling.

The playhouse looked the same. The lock still held the door closed. The broken window gaped. Inside, painted trees covered the walls. She could see no sign that Logan had been here.

The idea of going in again made her skin crawl. But what if Logan was in there? What if Pin had taken *him* inside the picture? She would try to trap him. Emily knew she would. She would keep him forever.

The girl had said she was lonely. She wanted someone. Probably even a four-year-old would do.

Emily ducked through the window. Her sneakers crunched across the glass.

"Logan," she called softly. And then a little more loudly. "Logan!"

She heard him again. "Emileeee!"

Or she thought she heard him. The call was so faint she might have imagined it. It seemed to come from far away.

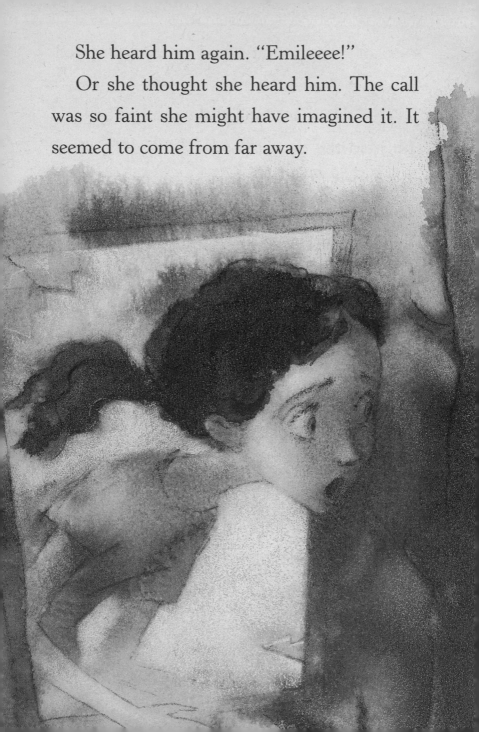

Where was he? Was he outside in the woods? Or was he inside the playhouse wall? How could she tell?

Emily stepped outside again. She ran from tree to tree. She heard "Emileeee" again. But the call sounded even farther away.

She stopped, holding on to the trunk of a tree. She stood still and listened. If Logan was out here in the real woods, she would hear him. He would rustle the leaves. He would snap a twig. Maybe he'd stub his toe on a root.

She heard nothing. The only sound was the light whisper of a summer breeze through the leaves.

Emily went back to the playhouse. She climbed through the window again. What choice did she have?

She couldn't leave Logan alone with that girl. She couldn't let her brother be lost inside a picture!

Emily stopped in front of the painted

picnic and studied it carefully. Had anything changed?

She could see the unlit campfire. She could see the food on the red and white cloth. The hot dogs, the mustard, the potato salad. She could see everything except the marshmallows. The marshmallows were gone. Every single one was gone.

Logan loved marshmallows!

"Emileeee!" The voice was still distant, but closer this time. It must be coming from inside the picture! She had no choice. She had to go in again.

But how had she done it before?

Emily moved close to the wall. She moved so close that when she raised her arms, her fingers almost brushed the surface. Then she closed her eyes and stepped forward.

She expected to bump into the wall. But

she didn't. She took another step. Then another.

When she opened her eyes, she saw trees everywhere. Painted trees. And all was silent again.

She took a deep breath. She'd done it! She was inside the picture once more.

But where was Logan?

8

A Flash of Red

Emily looked in the woods. She checked behind every tree. She looked under a weeping willow. She climbed over a pile of rocks. She couldn't find Logan.

Finally, she tried the playhouse door. The handle turned. The door swung open. She peeked in. Again, this playhouse was perfect. There was no broken glass on the floor. There was no Logan, either.

She walked to the wall on the opposite side. The picture was the same. It was the woods and another playhouse. The picnic lay beside it. The campfire was unlit. There were no marshmallows.

Then Emily looked more closely. The hot dogs were there. The mustard and pickles were, too. But the ketchup was gone.

Logan was a funny kid. He didn't like hot dogs, but he loved ketchup. Once Mom had caught him drinking it right from the bottle.

Clearly he had been here. Pin must have taken him into the wall twice. Maybe more.

Emily sighed. She squeezed her eyes shut and stepped forward. She didn't even lift her arms to protect herself. She just stepped. Then she kept on stepping.

When she opened her eyes, she was standing in the woods.

"Logan!" she called. She got no answer. These woods were much quieter than the real woods. No breeze stirred. No squirrels rustled through the leaves. No birds sang.

Why hadn't Pin's mother painted squirrels and birds? This place needed a little life. But if she had painted them, would they have come alive?

Emily shuddered. She didn't want to think about things like that.

She called again. "Logan!"

Would she have to go inside the playhouse and do it all over? How many pictures had he gone through? If they kept going deeper, would it be harder to get back?

That was something else she didn't want to think about.

So she didn't. She just opened the door and walked back inside the playhouse. She came over to the picnic in the wall again. This time the mustard bottle had been tipped over. It oozed yellow onto the cloth.

"Logan!"

She stopped to listen. Was that someone calling her name? She wasn't sure.

She closed her eyes and pushed through the wall.

And then when Logan wasn't there, she did it again. And again.

Once she caught a flash of red disappearing behind a tree. She had seen that red dress before. She heard a mournful voice, too.

"Sorry!" it moaned. "I'm sorry."

But Emily didn't care about anyone in red. And she didn't care about anyone being sorry, either. Logan was wearing blue. And Logan was never sorry for anything.

She went through the wall again.

She had begun to lose count. Had she gone through eight times or nine? More?

She spotted something blue. One of Logan's sneakers lay on the ground.

"Logan!" she yelled. She had been trying to stay calm. But she wasn't calm anymore. Her voice cracked.

Her little brother was a pain sometimes. Still . . . what would she do if anything happened to him?

And then . . . there he was, right in front of her. He was chewing on a ketchup sandwich. She could tell that's what it was. Ketchup had dripped onto his shirt.

The food here must be real if you stayed inside the picture. Emily hated to think how that sandwich would taste back in the real world.

"Hi, Emily," Logan said. He said it as if

meeting inside a picture were the most normal thing in the world.

He held out the sandwich for her to see. His hands were grimy. The bread was smushed. The ketchup oozed through. "Look," he said. "I'm having a picnic with Pin."

Emily hadn't even noticed Pin. She sat near Logan, grinning. But this time her grin didn't look friendly.

All Emily's worry burst out as anger. She grabbed Logan's arms and shook him. She shook him so hard he dropped the sandwich.

"What do you mean," she yelled, "running off like that? You could have been lost. Don't you know you could have been lost?"

Logan's face puckered. His chin quivered. Tears brimmed. "I didn't run off," he said. "I was looking for you. Pin said she knew where you were."

Emily turned on Pin instead. "Inside the playhouse? Inside playhouse after playhouse after playhouse? *That's* where you were looking for me?"

Pin shrugged. Her shrug was slow and lazy. It made Emily even more angry.

"You found us, didn't you?" Pin said.

Who did this girl think she was, anyway? Emily stepped closer so that they stood almost nose to nose. "Why did you kidnap my brother?" she demanded.

Logan tugged on her shirt. "It's all right, Emily," he said. "Pin didn't 'nap me. I didn't take a nap at all."

"Oh, Logan!" Emily cried. She scooped her little brother into her arms and hugged him tight.

She spoke past him to the girl. "We're going back. And you're not going to stop us."

Again, that slow shrug. Pin's shoulders rose almost to her ears, then dropped again. "Okay," she said. Her grin grew wider. "But how?"

That stopped Emily. How had she done it before?

She had just . . . She had just gone, hadn't she? She'd closed her eyes—

Wait. Had she closed her eyes? She had closed her eyes when she'd gone through the wall. But not when she left Pin. She'd just blasted through. Through Pin. Through the trees. Through all the fake stuff in this silly picture.

Could she do that again? She was much deeper inside the picture now.

Emily took a step forward. Logan was heavy. She couldn't run holding him.

Pin stood off at one side, watching. Her mean grin had faded. But she had an I-know-something-you-don't look.

Emily set Logan down. "We'll go inside the playhouse," she told Pin. "We'll just go back through the wall."

Pin nodded as if she agreed with the plan.

But she said, "Then you'll be even deeper inside."

Emily's scalp prickled. Pin was right. That was how she had gotten here. She had gone through wall after wall after wall. But how could they go through a wall backward?

Emily wanted to cry. She wanted to scream. She wanted to hit that smug girl standing there with her smug face in her smug sailor's dress.

"Would you like a ketchup sandwich?" Pin asked.

Emily started to say "No!" She definitely, certainly, absolutely did *not* want a ketchup sandwich. But a thought stopped her. *Where had the bread come from?*

There had been no bread in the picture before. Only hot dogs. And ketchup and mustard and marshmallows.

In one picture there had been graham crackers and chocolate bars for s'mores, too. But they had come later. Those things weren't in the first picture.

And that was when Emily put it together. Pin had said her mother was here. And Emily herself had seen someone in a red dress. Twice she had seen her. Emily had heard her say "Sorry," too.

So Pin's mother must be here. At least she was in one of the layers of the wall. She must have come back after she died.

And she was the reason the marshmallows had "toasted," too. She had made the bread appear as well. She was using the artist's palette and brush. The ones she had painted into the picture.

Pin's mother was changing the picture from inside. That was her way of saying she was sorry she had left Pin. But she was afraid to face the girl she had left so long ago.

If they found Pin's mother . . . If Pin wasn't alone anymore, she wouldn't need to keep Emily and Logan here. Maybe she'd even help them find their way out!

"Pin," she said, "I've got an idea."

9

Fire!

"What kind of an idea?" Pin asked. She wasn't smiling any longer.

"You know what you said before about your mother?"

"What?" Pin sounded cross. She didn't seem to like talking about her mother. "What did I say?"

"You said she's here. But she's playing hide-and-seek. You can never find her?"

"Y-e-a-h-h-h." Pin drew the word out. She was clearly waiting to see where Emily was going.

"Well, what if Logan and I help you look for her? If we all look together, I'm sure we'll find her."

Pin tugged on the red tie of her sailor dress. "My mother's been gone for a long, long time," she said. "Since before—"

She stopped. She didn't say before what. But Emily knew. Since before Pin had burned her father's house.

Emily stepped closer. "Did your mother like to wear red?"

Pin looked surprised. And then she looked as if she might burst into tears. She nodded. "She painted herself into the picture . . . the same time she painted me. She was mostly behind a tree. But you could see her red dress. It was my favorite. She wore it the day she—" She stopped, caught her breath.

"The day she went away?" Emily said softly.

Again, Pin nodded.

"Then I think I've seen her. Just a little while ago. Over there!" Emily pointed toward the trees where she had seen the flash of red.

Pin turned slowly to look where Emily pointed. "Over there?" she asked. She spoke softly, her voice filled with awe. Emily might have said she'd seen an angel in the trees.

She turned back to Emily. "Red? You said she was wearing red?"

Emily nodded. "And she said she was sorry. I heard her say she was sorry."

"Sorry?"

"For leaving you. I'm sure she's sorry for leaving you."

"Oh," Pin said. "Then let's—" Suddenly she went pale. Her gaze was caught by something behind Emily. She looked . . . well, the truth was she looked like a ghost! Or as if she'd just seen one.

"No!" Pin cried. Her hands flew up to cover her face. "No! Don't!"

Emily whirled to see what was wrong.

Logan! She hadn't been watching him. She'd been thinking about Pin's mother instead. He was squatting in front of the tepee of sticks. The sticks had waited years and years for a fire, but no more.

Logan must have had matches in his pocket again. And while Emily and Pin had been talking, he'd taken them out. He had struck one of them.

Flames licked at the sticks.

"Logan!" Emily cried.

He looked up. Guilt smeared his face like jam.

The bright flame leapt higher.

"Get away from there!" Emily cried. She ran, grabbed Logan's arm, and pulled him to her.

But even as she pulled Logan away, Pin began to scream. "Fire!" she yelled. "Help! Fire!"

Emily looked from Pin to the fire and back to Pin again. It was a very small fire. It was a small fire with nothing close by that would catch. And Logan hadn't been hurt. There was nothing to get so excited about.

"Pin," Emily said. "Don't—" But Pin was already running. She was running away.

Emily and Logan stood watching. "Look!" Logan said. He leaned against Emily's side. He slipped a thumb into his mouth. "Wook!" he said again around the thumb.

Emily looked. A woman in a red dress had come out from behind one of the trees. She stood waiting, her arms open.

Sobbing, Pin ran into them.

From where they stood, Emily couldn't

hear what the woman was saying. Somehow her heart could hear, though. "Hush," her heart heard. "Hush! It's all right. I'm here."

"Is that Pin's mommy?" Logan asked.

Emily could only nod, her throat tight.

For a long moment, neither Logan nor Emily moved. They just stood there, leaning into one another, watching. Pin's mother stroked Pin's hair and crooned to her. And Pin sobbed. But it wasn't unhappy crying. The tears seemed like pure joy.

Finally, the pair turned and moved away, holding hands.

When Emily saw they were really going, she caught her breath. "Wait!" she called. "Wait! You can't leave us here." She started after them.

She had gone only a few steps when they disappeared. They simply vanished among the trees. They had never even bothered to look back.

Emily turned to her brother. He gazed up at her with trusting eyes.

Poor little kid! He didn't understand that they were in trouble. Pin was all right now, but nothing had changed for them. They were still trapped inside this picture. And Emily didn't have any idea how they would get out.

She took hold of Logan's small, grimy hand. "Don't be scared, Logan," she said.

"I'm not," he replied cheerfully.

Emily sighed. Of course he wasn't scared. He didn't understand. He probably didn't even understand how strange it was to step inside a picture. Little kids thought that whatever happened was just the way the world was meant to be.

She squeezed Logan's hand. She had never felt so alone. She hadn't liked Pin all that much. But she liked being alone in Pin's painted world even less.

"I want to go home," Logan said.

"Me too," Emily answered. But her feet seemed to be glued to the ground. She had no idea what to do.

"Emily?" Logan sounded impatient. In a few minutes he'd probably start whining. Then he'd move on to tears.

"I'm thinking!" she told him. "Just let me think!"

But he wasn't letting her do anything. He tugged on her hand. He pulled her toward the campfire. Why was he so proud of that darned fire? He knew he wasn't supposed to be playing with matches.

Already the flames had begun to sputter

and die back. It had never been much of a fire.

"I want to go home!" Logan said again. And this time he broke away and ran toward the fire.

And that's when Emily saw it. The flames had burned a hole in the picture. The hole was big enough for a child to climb through.

It was big enough for two children to climb through.

The paint was black and bubbled around the edges. On the other side of the hole, a squirrel scolded. Leaves rustled in a light summer breeze. Emily had never heard anything so beautiful in all her life!

Thank you, Logan, she thought. And she hopped over the dying embers and followed her little brother into their own world.

Emily and Logan walked side by side through the woods. Neither of them spoke. They splashed across the stream. They crossed the clearing where Logan had collected violets. Emily even picked up the bunch of wilting flowers she found dropped at the edge of the clearing. Then they climbed the hill.

They came to the place where the trees stopped and the circle of houses began.

"Let's go help Mama," Emily said to Logan. She ran her fingers through his tangled curls. "Then after lunch and after your nap, I know something fun we can do."

"What?" Logan asked. "What can we do, Emily?"

"We can play in the forest creek," she told him. "What do you think about that?"

Logan gave a happy little skip at his sister's side.

Emily reached down and hugged him. "Isn't it nice to be home?" she said.

About the Author

Marion Dane Bauer is the author of more than sixty books for children, including the Newbery Honor–winning *On My Honor*. She has also won the Kerlan Award for her collected work. Marion's first Stepping Stone book, *The Blue Ghost*, was named to the Texas Bluebonnet Award 2007–2008 Master List. Marion teaches writing and is on the faculty of the Vermont College Master of Fine Arts in Writing for Children and Young Adults program.

Marion has two grown children and seven grandchildren and lives in Eden Prairie, Minnesota.

About the Illustrator

Leonid Gore emigrated from Minsk, in the former Soviet Union, in 1990. He has since illustrated more than twenty children's books in the United States. His artwork in such books as *Lucy Dove* (an IRA-CBC Children's Choice and a *Publishers Weekly* Best Book of the Year) and *Sleeping Boy* (a *Publishers Weekly* Best Book of the Year) has been widely praised. Critics have called his work "visually stunning," "brilliant," and "haunting."

Leonid and his wife, Nina, live with their daughter, Emily, in Oakland, New Jersey.

Read all of
Marion Dane Bauer's
ghost mysteries!

☆ Texas Bluebonnet Award Master List

The Blue Ghost

The light moved closer. It grew larger as it approached.

It had a shape now . . . or almost a shape. It seemed to form a person, a woman. One second Liz could see her clearly. She could make out the long, old-fashioned dress. She could see the woman's hair was pulled back in a bun. Then the figure wavered like smoke in a puff of wind.

The Red Ghost

Jenna pushed the blanket back again. She swung her feet out of the bed. But she stopped before she stood up. She just stopped and sat there, thinking.

The doll was in her closet, too. Miss Tate's doll. The one she was going to give to Quinn. It was all wrapped up, taped up, even decorated with a red bow. But it was in there.

And suddenly Jenna didn't want to open the closet door.